The Rusty Old Truck

By Mary Elsie Beall

Illustrated by Julian Arriola

PAGE PUBLISHING, INC.
New York, NY

First originally published by Page Publishing, Inc. 2014

ISBN 978-1-63417-135-9 (pbk)
ISBN 978-1-63417-136-6 (digital)

Printed in the United States of America

To growing readers Addison and Matthew,
and new truck lovers Emory, Walden, and Wyatt.

A rusty old truck came
rumbling down the road.

A green frog croaked
from a nearby log,

Be quiet, old truck, you'll wake all the bog!

But the noisy old truck kept rumbling along.

A yellow cat meowed from
a porch that was sunny,

You're rusty old truck, and you look so funny.

But the rusty old truck kept rumbling along

A red bird chirped from an apple tree,

11

But the ugly old truck kept rumbling along

A mother cow mooed from a barn painted blue,

We're glad you're here. We're waiting for you.

You're beautiful to us when you bring us hay.

For you know we are hungry at the close of day.

As the beautiful old truck was turning around,

Its rusty old horn made a very happy sound!

This "read to me" book uses the young child's interest in cars and trucks to enhance leaning in the following areas:

- primary colors
- different types of animals and their habitats and sounds
- descriptive words
- sense of rhythm and rhyme
- emphatic feelings

About the Author

Robert Lawrence, a young minister, and his bride, Nettie Lou Bradley, moved to his first church assignment in Citronelle, Alabama. Here they began a lifelong ministry to people, especially those in need during the depression. Before the end of the first year, their first child, the author, was born. In good southern tradition she was given two names and called by both. Mary Elsie was four years old when the first move occurred and although it was upsetting she had to learn to be uprooted and to meet new people every four years because the church denomination required an itinerant ministry.

This environment influenced her future choices of education and careers. She attended Huntingdon College in Montgomery, Alabama and became a Director of Christian Education after receiving training at Emory University. She served several churches before becoming the first Director of the Alachua County (Florida) Foster Grandparent Program. This federally funded program provides a package of benefits for low income senior volunteers who are placed in agencies that serve children with special needs. During the training of these individuals who are sixty years of age or older, some would share their regret that they hadn't helped their own children to become more sensitive people.

Mary Elsie Beall is now retired and living on a hilltop ranch in Alabama. She has enjoyed being with her two grandchildren as they have progressed from being little truck lovers to good readers. She is convinced that sensitivity and empathetic feelings have to be a part of early learning and she builds this into her writing for children.

CPSIA information can be obtained
at www.ICGtesting.com
Printed in the USA
BVHW021519030620
580777BV00004B/186